D0436161

Dear Parent:

Congratulations! Your child is taking
the first steps on an exciting journey.
The destination? Independent reading!

STEP INTO READING® will help your child get there. The program offers
five steps to reading success. Each step includes fun stories and colorful art.
There are also Step into Reading Sticker Books, Step into Reading Math
Readers, Step into Reading Phonics Readers, Step into Reading Write-In
Readers, and Step into Reading Phonics Boxed Sets—a complete literacy
program with something for every child.

Learning to Read, Step by Step!

Ready to Read   Preschool–Kindergarten
• big type and easy words • rhyme and rhythm • picture clues
For children who know the alphabet and are eager to
begin reading.

Reading with Help   Preschool–Grade 1
• basic vocabulary • short sentences • simple stories
For children who recognize familiar words and sound out
new words with help.

Reading on Your Own   Grades 1–3
• engaging characters • easy-to-follow plots • popular topics
For children who are ready to read on their own.

Reading Paragraphs   Grades 2–3
• challenging vocabulary • short paragraphs • exciting stories
For newly independent readers who read simple sentences
with confidence.

Ready for Chapters   Grades 2–4
• chapters • longer paragraphs • full-color art
For children who want to take the plunge into chapter books
but still like colorful pictures.

STEP INTO READING® is designed to give every child a successful
reading experience. The grade levels are only guides. Children can progress
through the steps at their own speed, developing confidence in their
reading, no matter what their grade.

Remember, a lifetime love of reading starts with a single step!

PRINCESS

STORIES

TO

SHARE

Step into Reading, Random House, and the Random House colophon are registered trademarks of Random House, Inc.

Visit us on the Web!
StepIntoReading.com
randomhouse.com/kids

Educators and librarians, for a variety of teaching tools, visit us at
RHTeachersLibrarians.com

ISBN 978-0-375-97302-4
Printed in the United States of America 10 9 8 7 6 5 4 3 2 1

STEP INTO READING®

STEP 2

PRINCESS STORIES TO SHARE

Step 2 Books

A Collection of Six Early Readers

Random House 🏠 New York

Contents

STEP INTO READING®

STEP 2

Disney
PRINCESS

A **Dream** *for*
a **Princess**

By Melissa Lagonegro
Illustrated by Pulsar Estudio

Random House 🏠 New York

There once was a girl
named Cinderella.
She was kind and gentle.

Cinderella lived with
her wicked Stepmother
and stepsisters.

She had many chores.

She served them tea.

She cooked their food.

She washed their clothes.

"Get my scarf!"

yelled one sister.

"Fix my dress!"

shouted the other.

They were very mean
to poor Cinderella.

One day,
a letter came
from the palace.
"Come meet the Prince
at a Royal Ball," it said.

The stepsisters
were very excited.
Cinderella was, too!

Cinderella dreamed of
wearing a fancy gown . . .

. . . and dancing with
the Prince.

Cinderella's Stepmother
gave her more chores.
Cinderella did not
have time to make
her ball gown.

"Surprise!"
cried her little friends.
They had made her
a fancy gown.

"Now I can go
to the ball!"
cheered Cinderella.

Oh, no!
The stepsisters
tore her gown.
It was ruined!

Cinderella cried.

Piff, puff, poof!

Her Fairy Godmother appeared.

"You cannot go
to the ball
like that," she said.

She waved
her magic wand.
Poof!

A royal coach.

White horses.

Two coachmen.

And a beautiful gown!

Cinderella was headed

to the ball!

At the ball,
the Prince saw
Cinderella.

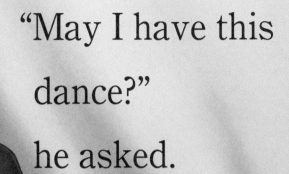

"May I have this
dance?"
he asked.

They danced . . .

. . . and danced . . .

. . . and danced.

Cinderella was so happy.
She was wearing
a fancy gown.

And she was dancing
with the Prince!

Her dream had come true!

The
Sweetest Spring

By Apple Jordan

Illustrated by

Francesco Legramandi & Gabriella Matta

Random House 🏠 New York

Spring is here!

There is much to do.

Sweep the floors
and mop up, too.

Clean the windows.

Scrub the floor.

Dust the tables.

Wash the door.

Singing makes
the chores more fun.
One, two, three!
The work is done.

The house is ready
to welcome spring.
Sharing the chores
is the sweetest thing.

Winter is over.
Now it is spring.
Ariel and her sisters
sing for the king.

Everyone gathers
to see all the flowers.

They dance and sing
for hours and hours.

The salt water is warm.

It smells of spring.

A springtime fair

is the sweetest thing.

Spring is here!
Jasmine has one wish—
to see a spring shower.
Splish-splash-splish!

Rain showers are

a sure sign

it is spring.

Splashing in puddles
is the sweetest thing.

Spring is here!

Wake up, friends!

The winter slumber
has come to an end.

A robin comes out
to sing a spring song.
The bumblebees are
buzzing right along.

The animals are happy.
At last it is spring.
Greeting our friends
is the sweetest thing.

Cinderella and her prince
share a spring stroll.
They see a rabbit
peeking out of its hole.

Flowers bud.

Roses bloom.

Wedding bells ring

for this new

bride and groom.

The happy couple shares
the wonders of spring.

Springtime love
is the sweetest thing.

Belle makes a garden.

There is much to do.

She wants plants
and pretty flowers, too.

She plants some seeds,
all in a row.

The soil
needs water.
It helps
flowers grow.

Belle waits . . .

and waits . . .

for days and hours.

The garden has grown
many pretty flowers.

The yard is filled with
the flowers of spring.
Planting a garden
is the sweetest thing!

STEP INTO READING®  STEP 2

Tangled

Outside
My Window

By Melissa Lagonegro

Illustrated by Jean-Paul Orpiñas,
Studio IBOIX,
and the Disney Storybook Artists

Random House 🏠 New York

Rapunzel is a princess
with magic golden hair.

One night,
Mother Gothel takes
baby Rapunzel!
She wants
Rapunzel's magic hair
to make her young.

Rapunzel grows up
in a tower.
Her hair
is very long.

Mother Gothel uses
Rapunzel's hair
to climb the tower.
Rapunzel does not know
that Mother Gothel
kidnapped her.

Rapunzel sees lights
in the sky every year.
She loves to paint them.
She wants to go
to the lights.

But Mother Gothel

says it is not safe.

Flynn is a thief.
Guards want
to catch him.
He must hide.

Flynn finds
Rapunzel's tower.
He can hide there!

Rapunzel finds Flynn
in her tower.
She is scared!

She catches him.
Then she hides him
in the closet.

Rapunzel still wants
to go to the lights.
She asks Flynn
to take her.

Then she will
let him go.
Flynn says yes.

Rapunzel leaves

the tower!

Mother Gothel cannot
find Rapunzel.
She thinks Flynn
kidnapped her.
Mother Gothel is angry.

Rapunzel goes to a pub.

She makes new friends.

She likes
the outside world!

The guards find
Flynn and Rapunzel.
Their new friends
help them escape!

Rapunzel and Flynn
find a cave.
Water fills the cave.
They cannot see!
Rapunzel uses
her magic hair.
It glows and shows
the way out.

Rapunzel sees the kingdom.

Rapunzel sees a picture.

It shows the King,

the Queen,

and the lost princess.

The Princess has

the same green eyes

as Rapunzel.

Rapunzel sees the lights!
She and Flynn fall
in love.

But Flynn sails away.

Rapunzel is sad.

She goes back

to the tower

with Mother Gothel.

Rapunzel learns that she
is the lost princess!
Mother Gothel
sent Flynn away.

Rapunzel wants to leave.
But Mother Gothel
will not let her go.

Flynn comes
to save Rapunzel!
He cuts her hair.
The magic is gone.
Mother Gothel turns
to dust!

But Flynn is hurt.

Rapunzel cries.

Her tears heal Flynn!

Everyone welcomes
Princess Rapunzel home.
They all live
happily ever after!

 STEP INTO READING®

Disney PRINCESS

The
Perfect Dress

By Melissa Lagonegro
Illustrated by Elisa Marrucchi

Random House 🏠 New York

Dust and dirt
make a mess!

Cinderella needs
a brand-new dress.

Clean and bright.

Oh, what fun!

This blue dress is
the perfect one.

Jasmine must choose
a skirt or a gown.

Her friend Rajah

looks on with a frown.

Jasmine and Aladdin
enjoy a starry night!

Her green outfit
is truly just right.

Belle is excited about
the fancy feast!

She gets dressed for
her date with the Beast.

Belle and the Beast
share a night of romance.

Her yellow gown is
perfect for this dance.

Everyone sings in
the wedding parade!

King Triton sends off
his little mermaid!

Ariel's wedding dress
fits just right.

Prince Eric thinks she
looks lovely in white!

Sleeping Beauty has
such a busy day!

The fairies can help.

They are on their way!

Music and menus.
There is much to do.

Should Aurora's dress
be pink or dark blue?

The Prince arrives with
his horse by his side.

Snow White must dress
for their royal ride.

It's chilly and windy.
It feels like a storm.

A blue and red cape will keep Snow White warm.

Slip on the shoes.

Fluff up the dress.

Put on the jewelry.

Look your best.

Which one do you think is the perfect dress?

Sealed with a Kiss

by Melissa Lagonegro
illustrated by Elisa Marrucchi

Random House 🏠 New York

Ariel and Flounder
love to play
hide-and-seek
under the sea.

They want the baby seal
to play with them.
Ariel points
to where the seal
could be.

The two friends
swim to find him.

They find the seal!

He is sitting

on a rock.

He cannot wait

to play hide-and-seek.

"One, two, three . . . ,"
Ariel starts to count.
The others hide.

"Ready or not,
here I come,"
she says.

Ariel looks
in the seaweed.
She searches
in the sea plants.

"Gotcha!"
cries Ariel.
She has found
Flounder!

Now Ariel
has to find
the baby seal.

Where can he be?

She looks

inside a chest.

She sees many things.

But no baby seal.

Ariel looks
under a rock cliff.
She sees
a sleeping blowfish.
But no baby seal.

Ariel hears music.
She sees fish
dancing and singing.
But no baby seal!

Ariel even goes
back to the rock.

She sees Scuttle.

But <u>no</u> baby seal!

Squeak! Squeak!

"What is that noise?"

asks Ariel.

They swim

to find out.

151

Oh, no!

It is the baby seal.

He is stuck!

His tail is caught

in a giant clamshell.

Ariel tries
to open the shell.
She lifts!
She pulls!

She does it!
Ariel sets
the seal free!

Ariel is happy
she has found
the seal.
And the seal
is <u>very</u> happy
to be found.

Ariel gives
her friend
a big hug.

She seals it
with a kiss!

STEP INTO READING®
STEP 2

Disney · PIXAR
BRAVE

A MOTHER'S LOVE

By Melissa Lagonegro

Illustrated by Maria Elena Naggi
and Studio IBOIX

Random House 🏠 New York

Princess Merida is late.
The royal family waits.

Merida's mother

is the queen.

The queen teaches Merida
how to be a princess.
She shows Merida
how to play the harp.
Merida is bored.

Merida wants

to play with her sword.

The queen tells Merida
she must marry
the son of a lord.

It is her job
as the princess.
Merida is mad!

Merida gets ready
to meet some lords' sons.
She wears a fancy gown.
The queen is proud.

Merida is sad.

She does not want

to get married.

The young lords
will shoot arrows
at a target.

The best shooter
will marry the princess.

Merida joins the game.

She is the best.

She wins!

Now no one
can marry Merida.
The queen is mad.

The queen wants Merida
to get married.
Merida says no.

She cuts
the family tapestry.

Merida runs away.
She meets a Witch.
She asks the Witch
to change the queen.

The Witch makes a cake
that holds a spell.
The spell
will change the queen.

Merida returns
to the castle.
The queen eats
the spell cake.

The cake
changes the queen—
into a bear!
Merida did not want this.

Merida and her mother
look for the Witch.
They need her
to break the spell.
But the Witch is gone!

Merida and her mother
go fishing.
They have fun.

Merida and her mother
meet a mean bear.
They run back
to the castle.

Merida wants
to help her mother.
She wants to mend
the family tapestry.

Merida tells the lords
she will marry
one of their sons.
The queen stops her.
She wants Merida
to be happy.

The men chase the queen
from the castle.

The queen is in trouble.

No one knows

she is the bear!

Merida protects her.

The mean bear returns!
The queen
protects Merida.
The two bears fight.

Merida fixes
the torn tapestry.
She and her mother hug.
The tapestry covers them.

The queen is
human again!
Love has
broken the spell.

Merida and the queen
will always be
mother and daughter.
Now they are friends,
too.